"He's Your Dog, Charlie Brown!"

“He’s Your Dog,

Charlie Brown!"

by Charles M. Schulz

SCHOLASTIC BOOK SERVICES
NEW YORK • TORONTO • LONDON • AUCKLAND • SYDNEY • TOKYO

ISBN: 0-590-08731-2

 This StarLine Edition is published by Scholastic Book Services, a division of Scholastic Magazines, Inc., by arrangement with The World Publishing Company.

30 29 28 27 26 25 24 01/8

Printed in the U.S.A. 07

"He's Your Dog, Charlie Brown!"

What do you do when everyone in the neighborhood is complaining about your dog?

Snoopy had certainly been acting up lately, and the kids were demanding that Charlie Brown do something about it.

"Why me?" he asked.

"Because he's your dog, Charlie Brown!"

That did it. Charlie Brown was forced into action, and he decided to write a letter to the Daisy Hill Puppy Farm.

DEAR DAISY HILL PUPPY FARM,
I AM WRITING IN REGARD TO ONE OF YOUR LESS DISTINGUISHED ALUMNI.

UNFORTUNATELY THIS ALUMNUS IS NOT LIVING UP TO MY EXPECTATIONS. THEREFORE, I AM GOING TO SEND HIM BACK AND HAVE YOU TEACH HIM A LITTLE DISCIPLINE.

"This is for your own good, Snoopy, and don't look at me like that. You have no one to blame but yourself."

LETTERS
U.S.
MAIL

"Now, one other thing... I'm going to call Peppermint Patty and make arrangements for you to spend the first night at her house."

"Hello, Peppermint Patty? Hi, this is 'Chuck,' you know... 'Chuck' Brown... Yeah... Well, I have a favor to ask. Snoopy is going back to school for a few days and he needs a place to stay tonight. Yeah, it's too far to make it in one day. Can you put him up for the night?"

"Sure, Chuck... Glad to oblige."

Now, the weird thing about Peppermint Patty is that she somehow has never quite realized that Snoopy is a dog. She has always been impressed by Snoopy's baseball playing and her enthusiasm has sort of blinded her.

They said good-by and Snoopy set off with his dog dish on his head and carrying his little suitcase. He was quite unhappy, a little frightened, and very mad.

Snoopy was really not in much of a hurry to get where he was going, so he meandered

down a few side streets,

kicked some tin cans,

and just took his time.

When he finally got to Peppermint Patty's house, he was greeted warmly.

"Hi, Snoopy, ol' pal! How's the ol' shortstop? It's good to see you again. Come on in, and I'll show you your room."

After Snoopy unpacked, Peppermint Patty fixed him a little snack in the kitchen. She was surprised when she saw him put his whole nose in a

bowl of cereal. "This is the strangest kid I've ever seen," she thought to herself. But that was only the beginning.

Now, Snoopy seated himself at a little table out in her backyard and really began to make a nuisance of himself. He leaned back in his chair and pretended that he was a World War I flying ace on leave in

Paris, and he snapped his fingers for service just as if he were in a little sidewalk café. Peppermint Patty was too polite to say anything and she brought him a glass of root beer.

This went on for three days. Snoopy swam in the pool, sunned himself in the yard, and snapped his fingers whenever he wanted something.

Peppermint Patty was getting a little worried. The dishes in the sink were beginning to pile up, and she was getting tired of waiting on this guest who was taking unfair advantage of her good nature. "I'll have to call Charlie Brown," she said to herself.

"Hello, Chuck? I don't know about this friend of yours here. He seems to think he's on vacation or something. I thought he was supposed to go to school."

"You mean he's still there?" cried Charlie Brown. "I'll be right over and get him!"

Charlie Brown grabbed a leash and set off across town. He hated the thought of putting a leash on Snoopy, but he could see no other way of controlling this dog who had gotten so out of hand.

And was Snoopy ever upset when Charlie Brown snapped the leash onto his collar and tried to drag him home!

Snoopy put on a wild performance pretending that the leash was strangling him. He coughed and he gasped, and he rolled on the ground.

Finally, he leaped to his feet,
gave the leash a great yank so that

it flew from Charlie Brown's hand, and ran back to Peppermint Patty's house.

"You're back again? Well, look, friend," said Peppermint Patty, "I'll let you stay awhile longer because I sort of like you, but let's get one thing straight. Around this house, everyone has to do his share. That's a family rule. You can stay with us if you want. You're perfectly welcome, but you're going to have to work! Did you hear me? Work!"

And Snoopy worked. Peppermint Patty had him doing dishes...

mowing grass . . .

washing windows . . .

vacuuming rugs...

and taking out the trash.

It wasn't long before Snoopy realized that he was caught between the leash and more work than he ever knew existed.

And when he got careless
and broke a dish, Peppermint

Patty banished him to the garage
for the night.

There's nothing worse than being banished to the garage.

Snoopy felt terrible. It was

dark, and for the first time in
his life, he knew what it was
really like to be lonesome.

Fortunately, Peppermint Patty had not locked the door, so Snoopy was able to sneak out, go into the house, gather all his things together, and run for home.

When Charlie Brown saw Snoopy at the front door, he threw his arms in the air and grabbed him.

They danced around and around. And when they went to bed, Charlie Brown said, "It's good to have you back, Snoopy."

Of course, they had to compromise a little. Charlie Brown agreed not to send Snoopy away and Snoopy agreed to try to act a little less outrageously.

The next day, Snoopy realized he had learned a good lesson.

"When it comes right down to it," he thought, as he stretched out under the bright blue sky, "dogs are born to sleep in the sun."